CAN I JOIN YOUR CLUB?

John Kelly

Steph Laberis

Kane Miller
A DIVISION OF EDC PUBLISHING

Duck wanted to make some new friends.
So he decided to join a club.

"Hello," said Duck. "Can I join Lion Club?"

"Well," replied Lion. "I see you already have a
magnificent mane. But can you **ROAR** like a lion?"
He took a deep breath, puffed out his chest and . . .

Duck gave it a try. He took a deep breath, **puffed** out his chest feathers and . . .

"Application **DENIED!**" said Lion.

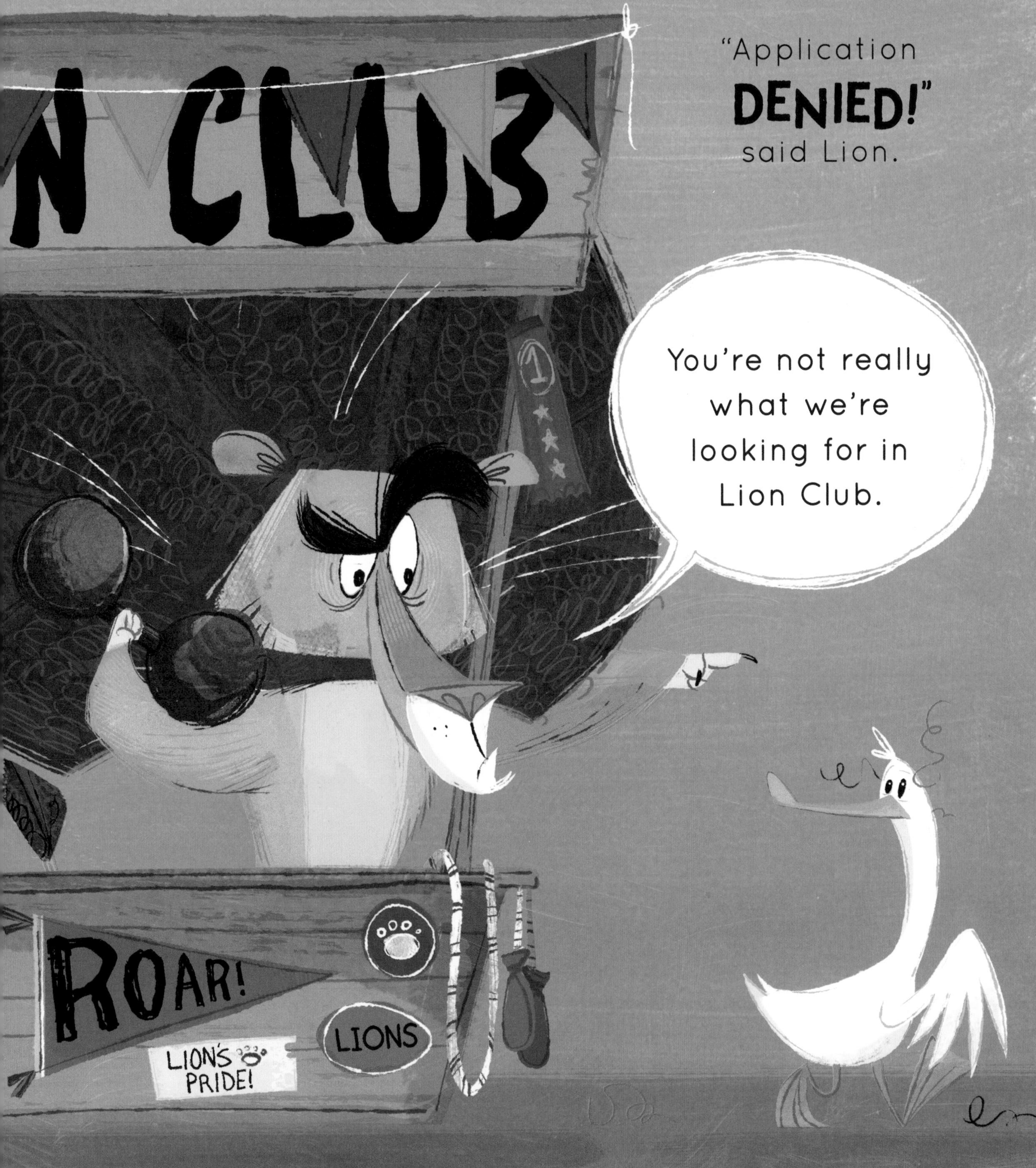

"Can I join Snake Club?" said Duck.
"Do you have any arms or legs?" said Snake.
"I've got legs and **WINGS!**"
smiled Duck proudly.

"That's a shame," yawned Snake.
"We don't really do arms, legs OR wings anymore.
Can you at least **HISS** like a snake?"

"Application **DENIED!**" said Snake.

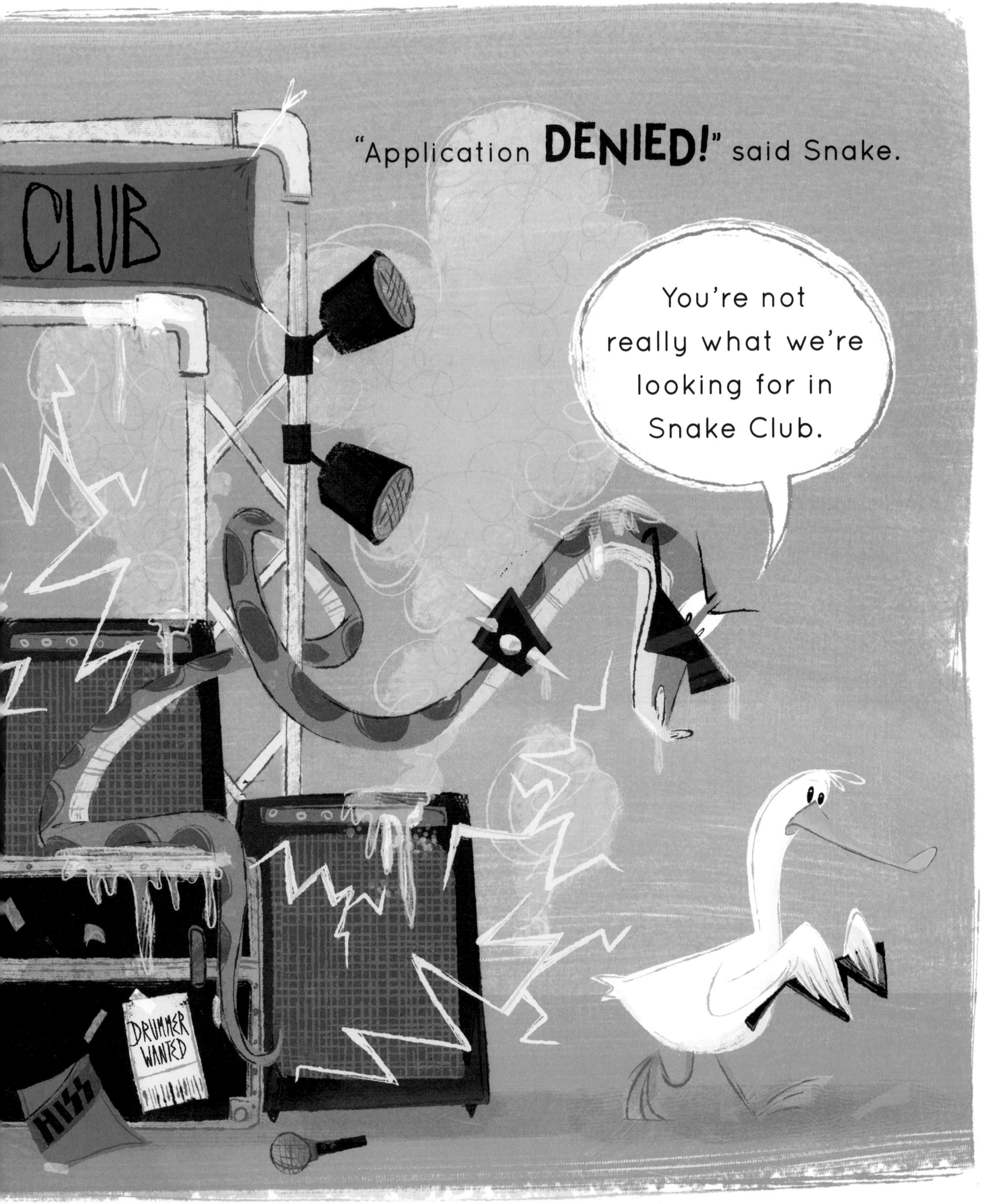

If you want to join our club,
you'll need the kind of brain
that remembers every single fact,
and can't forget a name.
If you study long and hard,
you'll grow intelligent,
and then you will be qualified
to join Club Elephant!
?

"Your turn," said Elephant.

"I'm sorry," said Duck, "could you repeat that?
I was distracted by your trunk waving around."

"Well," huffed Elephant, "can you at least
TRUMPET like an elephant?"

He took a deep breath, flapped his
big ears and . . .

Duck gave it a try. He took a deep breath, **flapped** his tail feathers and . . .

"Application **DENIED!**" said Elephant.

CLUB ELEPHANT

MATHLETE

You're not really what we're looking for in Club Elephant.

Duck felt down, but he knew what he had to do.

"Excuse me," said Tortoise. "Can I join Duck Club?"

"I'll have to ask you a question first," said Duck,
picking up his notepad and pen.
"Do you want to be in a club with me?"

"Yes, please," said Tortoise.

Duck put down his pen. "**APPLICATION . . .**"

Rabbit hopped up.
"Can I join your club?" she asked.

"Do you want to be in a club with us?" said Tortoise.

"Yes!" nodded Rabbit.

"Application **APPROVED!**" said Duck.

You are *exactly* what we're looking for in Our Club.

Soon **OUR CLUB** became quite popular.

And Duck let everyone in.
Because you can never have too
many friends.